P9-BUI-997

The Postcard Pest

OTHER YEARLING BOOKS
BY PATRICIA REILLY GIFF YOU WILL ENJOY

THE KIDS OF THE POLK STREET SCHOOL

THE BEAST IN MS. ROONEY'S ROOM

FISH FACE

THE CANDY CORN CONTEST

DECEMBER SECRETS

IN THE DINOSAUR'S PAW

BEAST AND THE HALLOWEEN HORROR

EMILY ARROW PROMISES TO DO BETTER THIS YEAR

MONSTER RABBIT RUNS AMUCK!

WAKE UP, EMILY, IT'S MOTHER'S DAY!

Plus, the Polk Street Specials:

WRITE UP A STORM WITH THE POLK STREET SCHOOL

COUNT YOUR MONEY WITH THE POLK STREET SCHOOL

THE LINCOLN LIONS BAND

MEET THE LINCOLN LIONS BAND

YANKEE DOODLE DRUMSTICKS

THE "JINGLE BELLS" JAM

ROOTIN' TOOTIN' BUGLE BOY

THE RED, WHITE, AND BLUE VALENTINE

THE GREAT SHAMROCK DISASTER

YEARLING BOOKS / YOUNG YEARLINGS / YEARLING CLASSICS
are designed especially to entertain and enlighten young
people. Patricia Reilly Giff, consultant to this series, received
her bachelor's degree from Marymount College and a
master's degree in history from St. John's University. She
holds a Professional Diploma in Reading and a Doctorate of
Humane Letters from Hofstra University. She was a teacher
and reading consultant for many years, and is the author of
numerous books for young readers.

For a complete listing of all Yearling titles, write to
Dell Readers Service, P.O. Box 1045,
South Holland, IL 60473.

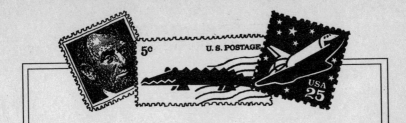

A POLK STREET SPECIAL

The Postcard Pest

. . .

Patricia Reilly Giff
Illustrated by Blanche Sims

A YEARLING BOOK

Published by
Bantam Doubleday Dell Books for Young Readers
a division of
Bantam Doubleday Dell Publishing Group, Inc.
1540 Broadway
New York, New York 10036

ISBN: 0-440-40973-X

Printed in the United States of America

Book Design by Christine Swirnoff

June 1994

10 9 8 7 6 5 4 3 2

OPM

To
Priscilla Wheeler,
a special person,
and
The Bookhouse,
a special children's bookstore

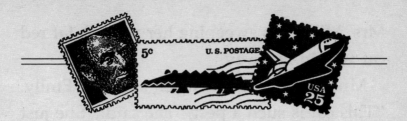

Chapter 1

Emily Arrow raced down the street. She was wearing her new orange-ice-colored shirt.

She had tried to curl the ends of her pencil-straight hair.

Today was a special day.

It was Postcard Day.

She passed her new neighbor's house.

Mrs. Mills was sweeping her path. A fat red cat was in her way.

Mrs. Mills laughed when she saw Emily. "This cat is such a pest," she said. "She just won't move."

Emily smiled. Then she saw Dawn Bosco up ahead.

Dawn had a new perm. Her hair was in neat "curly Qs" all over her head.

That Dawn always had something better than she did.

Emily caught up with her.

It was worse than she thought.

Dawn even had orange-ice laces in her sneakers.

"It's a special day," said Dawn. "Postcard Day."

"I know that." Emily sniffed a little.

Dawn sniffed too.

Jill Simon raced up to them. She was

wearing orange-ice bows on her four braids. "It's a special day," she said.

"I know," said Dawn. She looked at Emily and started to laugh.

Emily laughed too.

Sometimes Dawn was better than other times.

The bell rang.

They began to run. They raced through the school yard and charged up the stairs.

Ms. Rooney was standing at the door to Room 213. "Hurry," she said. "It's a special day."

Emily slid into her seat. She shoved her spelling book into the desk.

She pushed her lunch in too.

Then she leaned down to take a sniff. It smelled like cream cheese and jelly.

Good.

She had told her mother she wanted cream cheese and jelly every day for the whole month of May.

The cream cheese wasn't so hot, but she loved blueberry jelly.

Up in front Ms. Rooney was calling the roll.

Today she was calling fast. The class could hardly keep up with her.

Ms. Rooney couldn't wait to begin either, Emily thought.

A minute later the teacher looked up. "It's time," she said. She waved her hand at them.

Everyone rushed up to her desk.

Ms. Rooney had a pile of postcards on top. Some were green, others were blue. A few had red and yellow striped borders. There were even white ones with stars.

Emily shut her eyes for a moment.

She could almost see a girl finding her postcard in the mail. A girl far away.

Ms. Rooney and Mrs. Clark, the third-grade teacher, had traveled all over the country last year.

They had visited a skillion schools. They had brought back their addresses.

Now Ms. Rooney's class was going to write for pen pals.

Emily opened her eyes. She couldn't make up her mind which postcard to pick.

Would the faraway girl like a blue one—as blue as the sky?

Maybe she'd rather a white one with stars all over it.

Everyone was taking postcards.

"Don't forget to pick a stamp too," Ms. Rooney said.

Emily looked at the stamps.

She picked one with a baby deer.

Then she looked for a postcard.

Beast grabbed the last striped one.

Who cares? Emily thought.

Red and yellow stripes were horrible.

White with stars, Emily told herself. Definitely.

She reached out.

Dawn did too.

"Mine," Dawn said as she grabbed the last one with the stars.

Jill took the last blue one.

Emily was stuck with plain white.

She swallowed.

She thought about the faraway girl.

The girl would look at Emily's card.

She'd think Emily was as plain as her plain white card.

Emily sat down at her desk.

She wrote her name and address on one side.

On the other side she wrote:

I'm looking for a pen pal.

Up in front Ms. Rooney was collecting postcards. "It'll be a surprise," she said. "You'll have to wait to see where your postcard goes."

Dawn was dancing around with her star postcard. "Some kid is going to love this baby," she said.

She looked at Emily. "You picked white?"

Emily didn't answer. Pest, she felt like saying. Postcard pest. She had to smile to herself. She liked the sound of it.

Emily marched back to her desk and picked up her pencil.

She wrote on the bottom of her postcard:

Next time I write, I'll tell you a really speshal secret.

Chapter 2

Ms. Rooney's class marched down the hall.

They were on their way to the post office.

Mr. Mancina, the principal, waved at them as they walked past. "Don't lose anyone," he told Ms. Rooney.

Ms. Rooney winked at Emily. "I could lose a few people."

Emily laughed. She knew Ms. Rooney was teasing.

"Wait for us," Mrs. Clark called to Ms. Rooney.

Her class rushed up behind her.

Two kids opened the big brown doors.

Outside, it was windy.

"Whooo," Beast yelled. He held out his arms and made believe he was flying.

Emily had to laugh.

She didn't feel like laughing though.

Her postcard had a big lie.

She didn't know a special secret. She didn't know why she had written something like that.

She held on to her purse.

Everything was blowing around in the wind.

Drake Evans, the mean kid in Mrs.

Clark's class, was running around, tapping people, pulling hair.

He reached for Dawn's purse.

"Don't try it," said Dawn. "I'll punch you right in the breadbasket."

She turned to Emily. "I think I like the star postcards the best. Don't you?"

Emily looked at Dawn's face.

She felt like giving her a punch in the breadbasket.

Instead she made a fish face.

They turned the corner and went into the post office.

Pictures of stamps were hanging on the wall. Lions and tigers. Balloons and people.

The post office worker had known they were coming.

He told them about the first mailmen.

They had to ride on horses to deliver the mail.

He said it was dangerous work in those early days.

He even told them the names of some odd places where they had brought the mail. Places like Dead Man's Gulch and Hog's Glory.

Emily looked out the window. She could see two trees outside. They were covered with new green leaves.

If she crossed her eyes a little, the trees looked blurry. The dust on the window was sharp and clear.

She could see that Beast was crossing his eyes too.

He was crossing them at her, though, not at the trees.

They both began to laugh.

The post office worker cleared his throat.

Ms. Rooney cleared her throat too. She narrowed her eyes at Emily and Beast.

"Well," said the post office worker. "I guess it's time to get these postcards in the mail."

He began to look at Ms. Rooney's bags.

"Let's see," he said. "This pile is going to California. And this one to Ohio."

Drake Evans began to look through one of the bags.

"Watch out," said the postman.

Too late.

Postcards scattered all over the place.

"Good grief," said Mrs. Clark.

Everyone rushed to pick them up.

People were stepping on cards.

Emily knelt down to help.

She hoped Ms. Rooney would see—and forget about her laughing.

Next to Emily, Jill was scrambling around.

She was sniffling a little.

"Don't cry," Emily told her. "We'll get everything picked up."

Jill nodded. "But . . ." she started to say.

Emily wasn't paying attention though.

She was looking through the cards as fast as she could.

Yellow ones, blue ones, striped ones.

She found one white one, but that belonged to Noah Green.

She knew his skinny little writing.

Then Emily saw it—her own white postcard.

Quickly she asked Dawn for a pencil.

All she had to do was cross out the special-secret part.

"Sorry," Dawn said. "I don't have one."

Maybe Sherri Dent, Emily thought.

Before she could move, Drake Evans snatched the card from her hand.

He tossed it into the bag.

She reached for it.

Too late.

The postman picked up the bag and threw it over the counter.

Next to her, Jill was crying.

Emily felt like crying too.

Chapter 3

It was Tuesday morning.

Ms. Rooney reached up. She rolled down a large, colored map.

"This is our country," she said. "The United States."

Emily tried not to yawn.

It was hard to keep awake.

She had had a terrible dream last night.

It was a dream about her white postcard.

In the dream everyone was looking at her —looking and saying "Emily is a liar."

She had yelled "I'm sorry" as loud as she could.

No one heard her. No one even listened.

Then at last her father had come to the bedroom door. "You're just having a dream," he said.

She sat up to rub her eyes.

She wanted to tell him about the postcard and the lie she had written.

But he had patted her shoulder. "It's not very late," he said. "And you're hearing noises. It's Mom. She's upstairs in the attic looking for something."

Now in the classroom, Emily yawned again.

Ms. Rooney was pointing to a little triangle in the corner of the map.

"This is New York," she said. "This is where we live."

"How come it's pink?" said Beast. "We don't don't have pink grass . . ."

"Pink people . . :" Matthew Jackson began.

They were both laughing.

Emily yawned again.

"Don't be dumb," Dawn told the boys.

"All the different colors are to separate the states," said Timothy Barbiero.

What are states? Emily was going to ask. She was too tired though.

Besides, she had just thought of something.

What was her mother doing in the attic?

She almost never went up there.

Last night before Emily fell back to sleep, she had heard thumping and clumping.

Her mother had been moving boxes.

Emily tried to remember. Had her mother been singing something?

Emily yawned again. She must have dreamed that.

"The whole country is divided into fifty parts," said Ms. Rooney. "Each part is called a state."

"And we're New York State," said Noah Green.

"I used to live in Florida," said Dawn. "My grandmother still lives there."

That Dawn was so lucky.

Emily had lived every single day of her life on Stone Street.

And her grandmother lived in Brooklyn. It was about an hour away by car.

Emily made a fish face at Dawn.

It was a little fish face though.

She didn't want Dawn to see.

Then she thought of the car ride to her grandmother's house on Smith Street.

It always seemed to take forever.

And Dawn was saying it took three whole days to drive to Florida.

Emily was glad her grandmother lived in Brooklyn.

"Where do you think our postcards are now?" Beast was asking.

Ms. Rooney ran her hand over the map. "Some of them are on planes, going all the way across the country."

"How about that huge blue spot?" Sherri asked.

"That's the ocean," said Ms. Rooney.

"The Atlantic Ocean," said Timothy Barbiero.

Emily closed her eyes. That's where she

wished her card was—right in the middle of the ocean, where no one could find it.

Beast stood up. "Maybe some of the cards are in that green place . . . in the middle . . ."

Ms. Rooney put her finger on the map. "Here?"

Beast nodded.

"That's Colorado. *Col-o-RAH-do*," Ms. Rooney said slowly. "Huge mountains are there. Some have snow on top all year."

Emily was sick of looking at the map.

She wished she knew where her postcard had gone.

"I hope mine is over the ocean," said Jill.

Me too, said Emily in her head.

"Are you crazy?" Beast said. "Then no one will send you a letter."

"You'll never have a pen pal," said Dawn.

Jill raised her shoulders in the air. "I don't care."

Emily stared at her for a moment.

She tried to think why Jill didn't care.

She was glad no one knew that she didn't care either.

Chapter 4

It was Saturday. Pancake day. Emily's father was standing at the stove, turning them over.

"I hope your postcard goes to Alaska," Emily's little sister Stacy said. "It has snow, and ice, and an Eskimo girl might write back to you."

Emily reached for her orange juice. She didn't want to think about the postcard.

Maybe today someone would be getting it in the mail. The girl would be sitting down, getting ready to write to her.

Emily's father was saying, "If I had a postcard, I'd send it to California. It's right on the Pacific Ocean. There's no snow in the winter and . . ."

Upstairs, there was a thump.

Emily looked up.

Something crashed in the upstairs hall.

Emily's father went to the kitchen door. "Are you all right?" he called to Emily's mother.

Stacy leaned over toward Emily. "Will you lend me Delia My Darling's blanket?"

"I'm fine," Mrs. Arrow's voice floated down.

"Delia?" Emily asked.

"Your old doll. She has that wool blanket. She doesn't need a wool—"

"Why?" Emily wiped her mouth.

"Just because."

Emily raised her shoulders in the air. "I guess so." She thought for a moment. "I don't remember where—"

"Don't worry," Stacy said, grinning. "I took it already."

Emily laughed a little. "Pest," she said. But before she could say anything more, her mother appeared in the doorway.

She slid into her seat. "Don't you love pancakes?" she said to everyone.

Mr. Arrow slid a pile onto her plate.

"Guess what?" Mrs. Arrow said. "The junk room isn't the junk room anymore."

Emily thought about the junk room. Everything they didn't need was piled in there. Her mother's old sewing machine, Emily's kindergarten stuff, the winter boots . . .

"All the junk is in the hall now," said

Mrs. Arrow. "I'm painting the junk room . . ."

She stopped to take a bite of her pancake. "Mmm. What color do you think I should—"

"Purple," said Stacy.

"Definitely not white," said Emily. "Like a plain old postcard."

"Blue," said Mr. Arrow.

Mrs. Arrow smiled. "How about yellow? A nice, soft, happy—"

The front doorbell rang.

"It's not even nine o'clock," Mrs. Arrow said.

"Maybe it's the plumber," said Mr. Arrow.

It wasn't though.

It was Dawn Bosco. "Want to go to the store?" she asked Emily.

"I'll go too," said Stacy.

Emily mopped up the rest of the syrup with her last bite of pancake. Then she ran upstairs to get her money.

She couldn't walk through the hall though. The sewing machine was stuck in the middle. And boxes and books were piled everywhere.

Emily stopped to look at her first-grade raincoat and last year's Christmas dress.

Then she climbed over the sewing machine and took the money out of her dresser drawer.

Five minutes later, she and Dawn and Stacy were on the way to the store.

"What do you need to get?" Emily asked.

Dawn waved a dollar around. "Guess," she said.

"A bracelet," said Stacy.

"I can't guess," said Emily. Dawn always had everything.

Sometimes Dawn made her angry inside.

Dawn smiled. "Writing paper, of course. I saw some with butterflies."

"I'd get the rainbow kind," said Stacy.

"What do you think?" Dawn asked Emily.

Emily stopped to kick a stone out of her way. Maybe she'd tell Dawn she had her own birthday writing paper with her name on top.

She didn't even want to think about writing letters though.

"Get white," Emily said a little crossly.

Stacy pulled at the edge of her jeans. "Will you lend me money?"

Before Emily could answer, Dawn was talking again. "Yes," she said. "When someone answers my postcard I'm going to be ready. I'm going to get a stamp too. A gorgeous one with flowers or a heart."

Emily looked up at the trees. She hoped the stamp had fallen off her card . . . or maybe her postcard had gotten on the wrong plane. She hoped it was flying over the Atlantic Ocean somewhere. Somewhere far away.

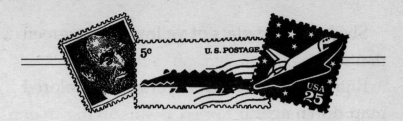

Chapter 5

It was Wednesday. Hot dogs for hot lunch.

Emily's favorite.

She was going to skip cream cheese and jelly for a change.

Too bad she looked like such a mess today.

She had brushed against the open yellow-paint can in the hall.

She had two splats of yellow on her green pants.

Right now, Ms. Rooney had the colored map down again.

"Has anyone received a postcard answer yet?" Ms. Rooney asked.

No one raised a hand.

"Well," said Ms. Rooney, "don't worry. It may take a couple of days."

She looked around at the class. "If your postcard could go anywhere, where would you want it to go?"

Noah Green raised his hand. "I was thinking . . ." he began.

Noah Green was always thinking, Emily told herself. He was the smartest kid in the whole world.

". . . about Washington, D.C.," he said. "Where the President lives."

Dawn Bosco stood up. "I was thinking

that too. My postcard had stars, just like in the United States flag. Someone in Washington, D.C., would just love it." She thought for a moment. "Wouldn't it be great if it went straight to the President?"

Emily made a face. "The President is too busy to be reading postcards," she said.

Emily looked across at Jill Simon.

Jill looked worried.

She was staring out the window.

Emily wondered what was the matter with her now.

Jill was always worried about something.

Just then the bell rang.

"Lunchtime," said Ms. Rooney.

"Hot dog time," said Beast. "I'm going to eat about a hundred."

The class started to get ready.

Emily grabbed her purse.

She rushed to get in line.

Jill was standing next to her.

Usually Jill talked a mile a minute.

She wasn't talking now though.

She had a droopy face. Even the tan bows in her hair were droopy.

Ms. Rooney's class was first into the cafeteria.

They rushed to the hot dog counter.

"I don't think I'm going to eat anything," said Jill.

Emily's eyes opened wide. Jill always ate more than anyone in the whole class. Maybe even more than Ms. Rooney.

"You'll be starving this afternoon," she told Jill.

Jill shook her head.

Emily went to get her hot dogs. She asked the lady to pile sauerkraut and mustard on top.

She reached for a container of chocolate milk.

Then she went back to her table.

A moment later the kindergarten class came in.

"What are they doing here?" Matthew asked. "I thought kindergarten went home at lunchtime."

Emily looked at the class.

Stacy was at the head of the line.

She smiled at Emily and waved.

They were best friends today. Emily had lent her fifty cents on Saturday.

"The kindergarten class is here to learn about the cafeteria," Emily said. She wondered why Stacy had needed the money.

Stacy said she'd have her head cut off before she'd tell.

Emily pulled some of the sauerkraut off her hot dog. She put it into her mouth.

It tasted wonderful.

Jill was looking at her. "I love sauerkraut," she said.

"Then why . . ." Emily began.

Jill didn't answer. She headed for the hot dog line.

A minute later she was back. She had two hot dogs with tons of sauerkraut on her tray.

"I have to eat, I guess," she said.

Emily leaned over. "What's the matter?"

"It's a secret," Jill said. "I can't tell you."

"Something special?" Emily said.

Jill shook her head. "It's a bad one."

Emily tried to think about Jill's bad secret.

Then she sat up straight. She had just gotten an idea.

What Emily had to do was find her own secret. A special secret.

Find one before someone sent a postcard to her.

Find one right away.

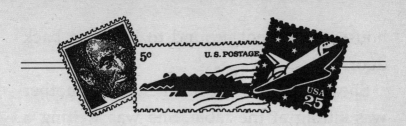

Chapter 6

It was Thursday. School was out early. The teachers had a meeting.

Emily stopped on her way home. She wanted to say hello to Mrs. Mills. "Where's your cat today?" she asked.

Mrs. Mills smiled. "Sleeping. All tucked up and cozy somewhere."

Emily nodded. She passed the next two

houses. She went around to her own back door.

She burst into the kitchen. Her mother was sitting at the table. She was writing a list for the store.

"Have some crackers and peanut butter," she told Emily.

Emily shook her head. "I spoiled my cream cheese record, remember? I had peanut butter for lunch. I'm going to have crackers and cream cheese."

Her mother laughed. "You've been eating a lot lately. I see all the bologna is gone from the refrigerator."

Emily shivered. "Not me. I hate bologna."

Her mother scratched at a spot of yellow paint on her cheek. "I thought Stacy hated bologna too. Maybe Daddy . . ."

"Where is Stacy anyway?" Emily asked.

"In the backyard, I think."

Just then the telephone rang.

"Be an angel," said her mother. "Get that for me."

Emily went into the hall and picked up the phone.

It was Dawn Bosco.

"I have the most exciting news," Dawn told her.

Emily looked up the stairs. She could see into the old junk room.

It didn't look one bit like the old junk room anymore.

It was all yellow now. And her mother had hung yellow and white striped curtains at the window.

"Guess . . ." said Dawn.

"What?"

"Guess what my news is."

"You found a dollar," Emily said.

"Nope."

Emily tried to think.

"It's about the mail," said Dawn.

"What?" Emily said again.

"I got a postcard," said Dawn.

"From California?"

"I don't know. I was so excited I didn't even look. It must have come from far away. It's filthy. The stamp is half on and half off. I wanted to call and . . ."

"Really?" Emily looked toward the table in the living room. She could see the mail in a neat pile.

"I couldn't believe it," Dawn was saying. "I looked on the table and . . ."

"Yes." Emily stood up on tiptoes to get a better look at the mail.

She couldn't see any postcards. Good

thing. She hadn't found one special secret to write about.

"Should I read it to you?" Dawn asked.

"Go ahead." If she reached out, Emily thought, she could almost touch the letters.

Maybe something for her was mixed in with the rest of the stuff.

"I was hoping for Arizona," Dawn said.

"Is that a girl or a boy?" Emily stretched the phone cord as far as she could.

"Are you paying attention? Arizona is a state. It has deserts and rocks and lizards."

The cord wouldn't stretch far enough.

Emily yanked off one of her sneakers.

She held on to the edge of the stair rail. She tried to push the letters off the table with her toes.

Dawn said something.

The letters slid off the table.

Emily swallowed. Suppose a postcard really was there?

"What?" she asked Dawn. She leaned over to pick up the mail.

"I don't believe it," Dawn said.

Emily started to flip through the letters. She could hear Dawn take a deep breath.

"Do you know what this says?" Dawn asked. "I'll tell you. It says, 'How would you like a punch in the breadbasket?' "

Emily stopped flipping.

Dawn sounded as if she was going to cry. "It's signed 'Drake Evans. Ha, ha.' "

Emily knew she was going to laugh. She bit at her lip. "He must have found your postcard . . ."

"In the post office," Dawn said. "And I even wasted my money on special writing paper."

Emily put her fist up to her mouth. She could feel her shoulders shaking a little. "Postcard pest," she said.

Dawn started to laugh. "You're right," she said. "But don't tell anyone. Don't tell one person."

"I won't," Emily said.

After Dawn said good-bye, Emily looked at the last of the mail.

Nothing for her.

Thank goodness.

Emily bent down to pull her sneaker back on.

Outside she could hear the sound of a car and the beep of a horn.

She didn't bother to tie the laces.

She ran to the window.

Her grandmother had just pulled into the driveway. She got out of the car, holding a box in her arms.

At the same time Emily saw something else.

A flash of color appeared at the back of the garage.

She leaned closer to the window.

For a moment nothing happened. She could see the trees with their new leaves moving in the breeze. She could see the purple irises standing in neat rows.

Her grandmother opened the back door. "No wonder you couldn't find those things in the attic," she told Emily's mother. "I had them all the time."

Emily had just enough time to wonder *what things?* Then she saw it again.

Stacy was poking her head around the side of the garage.

She looked around slowly and disappeared again.

Emily's mother was calling.

She didn't have time to think about Stacy.

She went into the kitchen to kiss her grandmother.

"Emily," her mother said. "I almost forgot. You have mail. A postcard. I put it on the counter so you'd see it."

Emily looked up. There it was. On the front was her name and address.

She turned it over. It was from the next town, Valley Stream.

It was from a girl. A girl named Carol.

She had written:

I want to be a pen pal.
I don't have anything special.
What's your special secret?

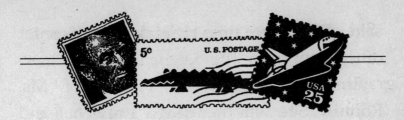

Chapter 7

Everyone was standing around Ms. Rooney's desk.

Ms. Rooney had pictures—tons of pictures.

"From my vacation," she said.

Ms. Rooney had gone across the whole country in her car.

There were pictures of her in a boat. "Here I am at the Mississippi River," she said. "That river runs right down the center of the country."

Emily looked at the picture of Ms. Rooney. She was wearing a straw hat and smiling. She was standing next to the water.

The water looked almost big enough to be the ocean.

Emily looked up at the colored map.

The Mississippi River was a skinny line wandering around in the middle of the country somewhere.

"Maybe someone will write to me from there," Sherri Dent said.

"Nobody is going to write to you from a river," Dawn said.

"Unless it's a fish," said Matthew.

"Dear Sherri Dent, I'm an eel," said Beast. "I live in the mud and eat junk."

"Gross," said Dawn.

"Silly," said Sherri.

Emily felt like laughing. But then she thought of Carol, her new pen pal.

Emily had gotten out her EMILY ARROW writing paper last night. She had started:

Dear Carol,

Then she had stopped. She didn't have one thing to say.

Emily looked over at Jill.

Jill was sitting in her seat.

She wasn't looking at Ms. Rooney's pictures.

She was staring out the window.

Emily went over to Jill's desk. "What's the matter?"

"Nothing," Jill said, and stood up.

She went over to the blackboard and wrote her name. "I have to get a drink," she told Emily.

Emily wrote her name too. She followed Jill outside.

"What's wrong?" she asked again.

Jill looked back at the classroom door. "It's a secret."

Emily leaned forward. "I won't tell."

Jill leaned forward too. "I told a lie."

Just then Stacy walked past. She smiled at them.

She stood in line ahead of them, waiting for a drink.

Stacy was yawning.

"Are you tired?" Jill asked her.

"I had to get up in the middle of the night," she said.

"You told a lie?" Emily whispered to Jill.

"I wrote a lie." Jill kept her voice low so Stacy wouldn't hear.

Stacy was listening though. Emily could tell.

Stacy leaned over the water fountain. But she wasn't drinking.

She was letting the water run across the side of her cheek.

"It was the postcard," Jill said. "I wrote something on the bottom."

Jill drew in her breath. "I said I was pretty."

She stopped for a moment. "Suppose someone writes to me? Suppose she asks me to send a picture?"

In front of them was an explosion of sound. It was Stacy, sputtering in the water fountain.

She was laughing—laughing hard.

Emily tried not to pay attention.

She looked at Jill.

Today Jill was wearing yellow bows on her braids.

Her eyes were big and brown.

"You are pretty," Emily said slowly. "You have a nice face."

Jill shook her head. "Look at these fat cheeks."

"I like them," Emily said. She was a little surprised at herself when she said it.

But she knew it was true.

"No . . ." Jill began, and stopped. "My father thinks I'm pretty," she said.

Emily was nodding.

Jill began to smile. "You really think I'm pretty?"

"I do." Emily shook her head up and down, hard.

Stacy wiped her mouth on the back of her hand. She rolled her eyes at Emily.

Emily shook her head.

Just then the classroom door opened.

Beast poked his head out. "Ms. Rooney

says it's time for math. She wants to know if you're drowning in the water faucet."

Emily took a quick drink.

She waited while Jill took a quick drink too.

Then they raced down the hall together.

At the classroom door, Jill reached out. "You're a good friend, Emily," she said.

Emily felt warm inside, happy—almost special.

She couldn't tell Carol that. She couldn't say "Jill thinks I'm a good friend."

It wasn't until she sat down that she thought of something.

What was Stacy doing up in the middle of the night?

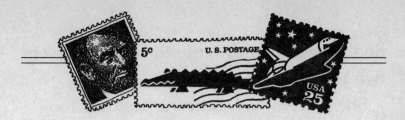

Chapter 8

Today four people had gotten post-cards.

Beast had gotten one from a teacher in New York City.

She said she could see the Empire State Building every day.

She said she was going to write to Beast every week.

"I knew I'd get a pest," Beast said. "I

don't have time to write to someone every two minutes."

Sherri Dent had gotten a postcard too.

"I have good luck," she said. "This comes all the way from a city called Houston, in Texas. It's from a girl named Rosalita." Sherri took a breath. "She says she always wanted a pen pal."

"Big deal," Dawn Bosco was saying.

Emily looked at Dawn.

Dawn stared back. "I meant it," she said. "It's nice to have a pen pal in Texas."

Emily finished her spelling page.

She looked out the window.

If only she could think of a special secret she could tell Carol.

"Finished, Emily?" Ms. Rooney asked. "How about finding Jim, the custodian? Tell him this window is stuck. Take Jill with you."

Emily stood up. She went out the door and down the hall with Jill.

It took a long time to find him.

He was outside under a tree. He was turning up the soil.

"It's for the Polk Street vegetable garden," he said.

"I didn't know we were going to have one," Emily said.

Jim grinned at her. "No one else knows yet either. It's my secret. I love good vegetables."

Emily sighed. "I wish I had a secret."

Jim turned over another shovelful of earth.

"Secrets are all over the place," he said. "You just have to open your eyes and look."

He pointed to the earth. "What do you see?"

"Dirt," said Emily.

"Stones," said Jill.

"Hmm," said Jim. "Better look a little harder."

Emily looked. All she saw was some dark brown dirt and a red worm.

"You really have to look around to find a secret," Jim said. He laughed and reached into his pocket. "One secret is Life Savers. Eat them before you go back to the classroom."

"Thanks," Emily said.

"Mmm," said Jill.

He winked. "Some secrets you don't want to tell."

"Right," said Emily.

"I'll show you one though. Stand still. Don't move."

On the branch right above them was a robin.

Emily didn't even breathe.

A moment later, the robin swooped down.

It grabbed the worm and flew back up to the tree.

"Now watch," said Jim. "Really see."

Emily watched.

The bird was watching too. It turned its head from one side to the other.

Then it hopped up. One branch. Two.

"A nest," Emily said.

"Baby birds," said Jill.

"Told you," Jim said. "Secrets all over the place. You just have to look and you'll find them."

Emily went back inside. The Life Saver felt sweet on her tongue. Lemony.

Then she stopped still in the hall.

For a moment she stood there, thinking.

She thought of a secret.

She took a step.

And maybe something else.

Two secrets.

Ms. Rooney popped her head out the door. "You two are taking forever. And where's Jim?"

"We forgot." Emily looked at Jill. "We forgot to tell him."

Ms. Rooney shook her head a little. She was smiling though. "It's spring," she said.

"One minute," Emily said. She headed back out the door with Jill as fast as she could.

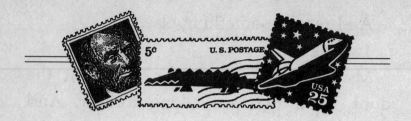

Chapter 9

Emily couldn't wait for the afternoon to be finished.

She couldn't wait to get home.

Mrs. Clark popped her head in. "Someone in my class just received a letter from New Jersey. Right across from New York," she said. "That's where I was born."

Ms. Rooney laughed. "That must have been a hundred years ago."

"Two hundred," said Mrs. Clark.

Ms. Rooney was standing at the map. "I'm showing everyone Rhode Island," she said. "It's right next to the Atlantic Ocean."

"It's the smallest state," said Mrs. Clark. She waved and went back out the door.

Ms. Rooney nodded at the class. "The biggest state is Alaska," she said.

Dawn Bosco leaned over to Emily. "Why are you smiling to yourself?"

Emily didn't want to say "It's a secret." Dawn would want to know what it was.

And Emily wasn't sure about it herself.

Not exactly.

Well, almost.

She felt a shiver of excitement.

"Emily?" Dawn asked.

She raised one shoulder. "Just happy," she said.

If only the bell would ring.

And then it did.

Emily was out the door in two seconds.

She raced down Stone Street. She tore up the driveway and into the yard.

She stopped before she got to the garage. "Stacy?" she called.

For a minute there was no answer.

Then she saw Stacy's head appear slowly around the garage wall. "What?"

"Can I come back there?"

Stacy shook her head. "No."

Emily took a step. "Please?"

Stacy looked as if she was going to cry. "You'll tell. Mrs. Mills said not to tell anyone."

Emily took a breath. "No, I won't. Cross my heart."

"Tiptoe then," said Stacy. "Everyone's asleep."

Emily tiptoed.

In the tall grass was a cardboard box. Inside was one mother cat and two kittens. They were curled up on Delia My Darling's blanket.

"The gray one is mine," said Stacy.

"Mom will never—"

"Yes she will. She said I took good care of them. She said anyone who gets up in the middle of the night to make sure everyone's all right . . ." Stacy stopped for a breath. "Anyone who takes time to feed them bologna . . . and borrow fifty cents for a cat toy . . ."

"It's Mrs. Mills's cat," said Emily.

Stacy nodded. "Mrs. Mills says cats always pick their own special place for kittens."

She raised her shoulders in the air. "This

cat picked this spot behind the garage. And we can't move them until the kittens are bigger."

Emily smiled. She touched the gray kitten's ear. "What will you name her?"

"Maybe Pest," said Stacy, laughing. "This cat is always climbing all over me."

Emily smiled. She stood up. "I have to see Mom."

She went across the backyard, opened the kitchen door, and called, "Mom?"

"Upstairs," her mother answered.

Emily took the stairs two at a time.

Her mother was in the old junk room— the yellow room now.

She was standing near the window with a tiny paintbrush in her hand. "Balloons," she said.

Emily couldn't stop smiling. Her mother

had painted a bunch of balloons on the wall. Pink ones and blue ones.

"Even a white one," Emily said.

They were tied with a painted pale-green ribbon.

"Gorgeous," Emily said.

Her mother nodded.

"About that box," Emily said.

"The one that Gram brought?" her mother asked.

"Yes," Emily said. "I remembered."

Her mother was nodding.

Emily sank down on the floor. "My baby clothes . . . and Stacy's."

Her mother reached out. She touched the top of Emily's head. "We're going to use them again," she said.

"Jim was right," said Emily. "There are secret things happening all over the place."

Her mother laughed. "I guess you could

call this a Thanksgiving secret. We have to wait for it until then."

Emily stood up. She was going into her room for that writing paper. She already knew what she'd write to Carol.

Dear Carol,

There are secrets all over the place. You just have to look for them.

I found out that my freind Jill is pretty. I think it's because she's nice.

I found out about new kittens—and my sister Stacy is going to keep one for us.

But the best thing of all is, we're having a new baby at my house at Thanksgiving.

Love from your new freind,
Emily Arrow

ALL ABOUT STAMPS

The Story of Stamps

"**W**e're lucky to have this." Ms. Rooney held something in her hand.

Beast knelt up on his seat to see.

It was just a stamp.

A plain stick-to-a-letter kind of stamp.

He slid down in his seat again.

"Suppose you wanted to write to some-one in the olden days . . ." Ms. Rooney be-gan.

"To a caveman?" Noah asked.

Ms. Rooney nodded. "At first there was no paper. People had to carve their letters on . . ."

"Stone," said Timothy. "I read about that."

Beast closed his eyes. He tried to think about scratching letters into a stone.

It was a good thing he didn't like to write letters anyway.

"When the letter was ready," asked Ms. Rooney, "how could you mail it?"

Beast opened his eyes. "You couldn't mail a stone."

"Even after people used paper," Timothy

said, "it was hard to get a letter to someone."

"Pigeons," said Noah.

"Coo coo," said Matthew.

"What?" Beast asked.

"People tied letters to pigeons," Timothy
said. "Then . . ."

"Vroom," said Matthew. "Into the air."

"They used camels for a while in the
1800s," said Dawn. "And reindeer in
Alaska."

"And what about horses in the Pony Express days," said Noah. "It took a long time.
The roads were bad. And it was dangerous
too."

Beast drew a Pony Express rider on a
horse.

The rider had a huge mustache.

Beast put in clouds of dust.

He put in a bunch of bandits.

"I guess it cost a lot of money too," said Emily.

"The thing was," said Ms. Rooney, "everyone who delivered mail was charging a different amount."

Ms. Rooney held up the stamp again. "But then . . ."

"I know," said Noah. "The Penny Black."

Ms. Rooney clapped her hands together. "Exactly right. Tell the class."

Noah stood up. "It was in England," he said. "In 1840. Someone thought about paying for mail with stamps. And the first stamp was . . ."

Beast guessed what he was going to say.

"The Penny Black," he said under his breath.

He liked the sound of it.

"It cost a penny," said Noah. "It was black and white. It had a picture of a queen."

Ms. Rooney kept nodding. "Then in our own country we made our first stamps."

"I bet I know whose picture was on it," said Beast.

"Who?" asked Dawn.

"James Polk," said Beast.

"Guess again," said Dawn. "It was George Washington on a ten-cent stamp. And Benjamin Franklin on a five-cent stamp."

Emily rolled her eyes.

Beast knew what she was thinking.

Dawn was a pain sometimes. She acted as if she knew everything.

Beast didn't even know who Benjamin Franklin was.

Dawn looked at him. "Benjamin Franklin was the head of the post office in the 1700s."

Ms. Rooney began to pass stamps around.

Beast got one with a flag.

"Look at it hard," said Ms. Rooney.

Beast looked hard. He saw numbers that told how much it cost. He saw USA, the country's name.

My father told me about a famous stamp," Alex Green said. "It's called the Inverted Jenny. Someone paid a ton of money for one a little while ago."

"What's *inverted*?" Matthew asked.

"Upside down," said Alex.

"What's . . ." Beast began.

Alex sighed. "Let me tell you. Jenny was a plane. The printers made a mistake. They printed the plane upside down."

"Someone paid a pile of money to mail a letter with a messed-up stamp?" Beast asked.

"Don't be dumb," Dawn told him. "It's a stamp to save. It's different. Unusual."

Beast drew a stamp with a picture of Dawn.

She looked like a rabbit.

He began to laugh.

Too bad it didn't have glue on the back.

He'd stamp it on Dawn's forehead.

He'd mail her off in an inverted Jenny.

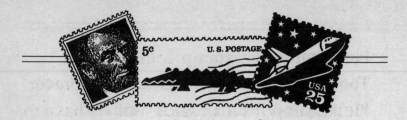

Starting a
Stamp Collection

"**G**reat news," said Ms. Rooney.

"No school tomorrow?" Beast asked.

Ms. Rooney shook her head. "We're going to have a class hobby."

"I hope it's cooking," Jill said.

"Detective work," said Dawn.

"I'll bet it's stamp collecting," said Timothy. "That's the biggest hobby in the world."

Beast bet it was stamp collecting too.

They'd been talking about stamps forever.

"It'll be easy," Noah said. "All we have to do is check the mailbox every day . . . and get everyone to save stamps for us."

Beast thought for a minute. "I'm going to ask at the ice cream store. They probably get lots of mail. And I'm always there anyway."

"There are plenty of places to get stamps," Ms. Rooney said. "You can buy them at the post office. You can try a hobby shop, and there are dealers . . ." She stopped for a breath.

Timothy nodded. "Stamp dealers are people who sell stamps that are worth a lot of money."

"Like that Inverted Jenny," said Alex.

Ms. Rooney smiled. "Right again. Now here's what we'll do. We'll gather stamps.

We'll put the ones we like in a special book. It's called a stamp album."

Jill looked as if she was going to cry. "I'm never going to get the stamps off the envelopes," she said.

"Don't worry," Timothy said. "I know how to do that."

"Me too," said Noah. "Drop the stamp

into water. After a while, the paper will float. The stamp will sink."

"Swish swish," Beast said.

"You can take the stamp out with tongs or tweezers," Timothy said. "You have to be careful not to tear the stamp."

"I'd never tear a stamp," Dawn said. "If you take good care of old stamps, they may be worth money someday."

"Like . . ." Alex began.

"The Inverted Jenny," everyone said.

Ms. Rooney put her hand up. "Remember . . ."

Everyone knew what she was going to say too. "Clean hands."

Beast looked out the window. "I think I'll save President stamps. Maybe I can find one with President Polk."

"Not me," said Jill. "I'm going to save . . ."

"I know," Timothy said. "Stamps with food."

"Pizza," said Jill.

"How about holidays?" Noah said. "Fourth of July and . . ."

"Animals," said Beast. "Tigers and elephants."

Ms. Rooney raised her hands in the air. "You can collect almost anything. Trains and planes, flowers and dolls, rainbows and birds . . ."

Ms. Cara, the art teacher, poked her head in the door.

"We're doing stamp albums," Ms. Rooney said.

"Good," said Ms. Cara. "Move the stamps around on the album page. When they look just right, mark the spot lightly with a pencil. Then attach the stamp with a hinge."

"Never paste them," said Timothy.

Jill's face was red. "I don't even know what a hinge is."

"It's a little piece of paper," said Ms. Rooney. "It has glue on one side. You fold it so one side is longer than the other. Wet the short side and stick it to the stamp. Wet the long side and stick it to the album page."

"Simple," said Ms. Rooney.

"Now all I need is an album," said Jill.

Ms. Rooney laughed. "It's right in back of this book. So let's get started."

5¢   U. S. POSTAGE   USA 25

Words About
Stamp Collecting

Album *(AL bum)*	A book to hold your stamps.
Collector *(kuh LEC ter)*	One who brings things together. A stamp collector finds stamps. He brings them together.

Cancellation mark *(can sell A shun)*	The post office prints lines over a stamp to show the letter has been sent. When you see these lines, you know you can't use the stamp again.
Condition *(con DISH en)*	Is the stamp new and clean? Is it old and messy? Stamp collectors pay more if the stamp looks perfect.
Design *(dih ZINE)*	What does the stamp look like? Does it have a picture of a person? A flower? A flag?

Foreign *(FOR in)*	A stamp from another country.
Hinge *(HINJ)*	A small strip of paper that has glue on one side. It is used to attach a stamp to an album page.
Perforation *(per for A shun)*	Holes are made between the stamps so they can be separated.
Sort *(SORT)*	To put into different groups.

Stamp	A small piece of paper
(STAMP)	to stick to letters and
	packages. People pay
	for stamps so the mail
	can be sent.
Valuable	A stamp that is worth
(VAL you a bəl)	money.

If you want to know more about the mail, or about stamps, be sure to visit your library. Look in the card catalogue under postage stamps or philately (stamp collecting).

The post office is another place for information. Stop in and ask them about beginning kits for stamp collectors.

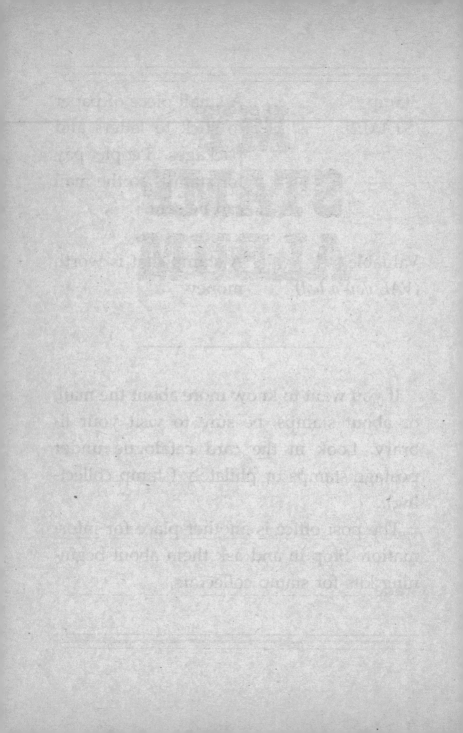

MY STAMP ALBUM

Name_____

Age_____

Grade_____

My favorite
stamp

My most colorful
stamp

My strangest
stamp

My state's
stamp

My favorite
flag stamp

My favorite
sports stamp

FAMOUS
PEOPLE
STAMPS

My favorite famous
person stamp

ANIMAL
STAMPS

My favorite animal stamp

FLOWER STAMPS

My favorite flower stamp

HOLIDAY
STAMPS

My favorite holiday stamp

STATE
STAMPS

My favorite state stamp

ALL KINDS
OF STAMPS